Little Goose

by
DAVID MRÁZ

Illustrations by
MARGOT APPLE

TRICYCLE PRESS
Berkeley

All rights reserved. Published in the United States by Tricycle Press, an imprint of the
Crown Publishing Group, a division of Random House, Inc., New York.
www.crownpublishing.com
www.trieyclepress.com

Library of Congress Cataloging-in-Publication Data

Mraz, David, 1947–
    Little Goose / by David Mraz ; illustrated by Margot Apple.
        p. cm.
    Summary: Little Goose tries to figure out what round things remind him of
as he makes his way around the pond.
[1. Geese—Fiction. 2. Mother and child—Fiction. 3.
Animals—Infancy—Fiction.] I. Apple, Margot, ill. II. Title.
    PZ7.W72843Lit 2007
    [E]—dc22

                                    2006017388

ISBN 978-1-58246-190-8
Printed in China

Design by Barbara Grzeslo and Betsy Stromberg
Typeset in Hadriano and Kairengu
The illustrations in this book were rendered in colored pencil.

11 10 9 8 7 6 5 4 3 2

First Edition

For Barbara, Casey, Jessica, John, Cindy, and the rest of my family flock;
and especially for my little goose, Max. —D.M.

For everyone in Rowe, Massachusetts . . . including the geese. —M.A.

Little Goose liked pebbles and puddles, marbles and bubbles, baskets and buckets and balls that roll. He liked the number **8** and the letter **o**, and how all those things made his eyes go walking, 'round and 'round without ever stopping.

"What is it about those things?" he wondered.

Off he waddled to find his mother. She was sitting by the pond, in the sand and the sedge at the water's edge.

"**Honk!**" she said.

"**Hoinkle-oinkle,** Mama!" he said in his little goose voice.

"Things that make my eyes go walking remind me of something, the way they go 'round and 'round without ever stopping. It's something cozy and comfy and happy, too. I've tried to remember what it is, but I can't. Can you?"

"I think you are the only one who can do that," said his mother.

Little Goose clacked his beak.

"I'll find out what it is," he said. "Even if I have to go around the world."

Mama Goose waved a wing over the pond. "The world is a big place," she said. "But if you keep one wing over water, your wing and the water will bring you home to me, safe as ever."

So Little Goose began his trip around the world, always keeping one wing over water. He waddled along and he wiggled along. And with a waddle and a wiggle, he came upon Turtle, dozing on top of his rock, in the middle.

"**Hoinkle·oinkle,** Turtle!" said Little Goose. "Things that make my eyes go walking remind me of something. Something cozy and comfy and happy, too. But I don't know what it is. Do you?"

"My little rock makes me comfy and happy," said Turtle.

Little Goose hopped onto Turtle's rock. He climbed up and up 'til he reached the top.

When he tried to sit, he slipped . . . and he flipped—**kerplop!**—into the water!

"That was not cozy or comfy or happy," said Little Goose.

"Maybe," said Turtle, "you're looking for something less slippery."

So Little Goose set off again.

He jigged along and he jogged along. And with a jig and a jog, he came upon Frog, sitting on a log, in the mud by the pond.

"**Hoinkle-oinkle,** Frog!" said Little Goose. "What do you know about hoops and hats and wheels that roll? They remind me of something, the way they go 'round and 'round without ever stopping."

"Well," said Frog, with a little hop, "flies go and go and they never stop."

Little Goose's eyes followed the flies, 'round and 'round. But he was not cozy or comfy or happy—he was dizzy!

"Maybe," said Frog, "buzzing things are not what you are looking for."

So Little Goose started off again.

He went slipping along and he went sliding along. And with a slip and a slide, he came upon Mouse by the water near her house.

"**Hoinkle-oinkle,** Mouse. Can you help me find something round that makes my eyes go walking?"

"My little house," said Mouse, "is round. And there's a hole at the top that goes into the ground."

Little Goose squeezed through the hole and pushed his way down into Mouse's house, far, far below.

But that tiny little house, just right for a mouse, was much too small for Little Goose. He was not cozy or comfy or happy in there.

"Mama?" he said.

But all he could hear was his own heart beating.

Poor Little Goose scrinched and scrunched.
Backwards he went, until at last he was out . . .
out in the air with the sky and the water.

"Honk!" he said, with a big goose sound!
"Honk!" he cried again, even louder.

He hurried along and he scurried along. And with a hurry and a scurry he was back—**just like that!**—to his home by the pond.

Little Goose ran to his mother. He was happy to be home, and happy to **honk** with a big goose sound.

"Did you remember," said his mother, "what it was? Have you found what things that go 'round remind you of?"

And all at once he knew.

It was his mama's wings, soft as ever. They made him cozy and comfy and happy all over, from side to side and bottom to top. They went 'round and 'round him, and they never stopped.